AROUND THE WORLD
IN 80 DAYS

JULES VERNE

PLAYMORE
PUBLISHERS

Editor: Heather Hammonds
Cover Illustration: Terry Riley
Illustrations: Terry Riley
Typesetting: Midland Typesetters

Around the World in 80 Days
First published in 2008 by
Playmore Inc., Publishers,
58 Main Street, Hackensack, N.J. 07601

Printed in China

The Author
Jules Verne (1828–1905)

Jules Verne was one of the most popular writers of his time and has sometimes been called the father of science fiction.

Born in Nantes, France, Verne's father was a lawyer and his mother came from a family of ship builders and seafarers. He was fascinated with travel from an early age and even tried to run away to sea when he was twelve. He studied law in Paris as a young man, but he soon gave up his studies to concentrate on his first love — writing.

The author of more than one hundred exciting novels, plays, and short stories, Verne accurately predicted many future scientific inventions and events, such as submarines, guided missiles, and space travel. He keenly studied the scientific discoveries of the time and wrote about them in many of his books.

Other successful novels by Verne included *From the Earth to the Moon*, *Journey to the Center of the Earth*, and *20,000 Leagues Under the Sea*, to name just a few.

Contents

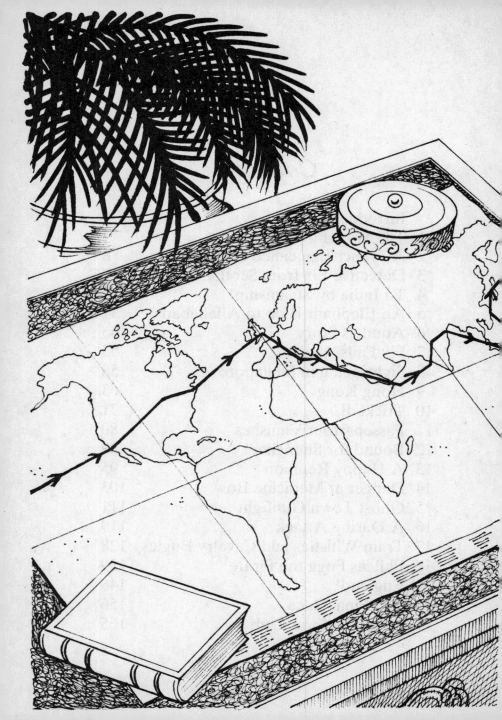

Introduction
The World of Phileas Fogg

The nineteenth century world of Phileas Fogg, the hero of this story, was very different from our own.

Today we fly at hundreds of miles an hour to the other side of the world in less than a day. In Phileas Fogg's time the world was lit by gaslight, and only the richest people could travel by steam trains, or slow, ocean-going steamships. Travel could be a very dangerous business, too.

Travelers had no telephones of any kind. The hi-tech communication system of the day was the telegraph, a chancy system where electronic messages could be sent around the world by overland wire and ocean cable.

In many ways, Phileas Fogg's nineteenth century journey was as big a venture as a space mission would be today. Traveling around the world in eighty days would have made him as famous as any astronaut.

Chapter 1
The Wager

Mr. Phileas Fogg, a member of London's exclusive Reform Club, had just finished reading a report in the Times newspaper. It was a story about a devilishly cunning robber who had stolen fifty-five thousand pounds from the Bank of England.

Mr. Fogg put down his newspaper with a sigh.

"Where can the bank robber hide now?" he said, settling back into one of the club's comfortable leather armchairs. "The man's stolen fifty-five thousand pounds in used banknotes from the Bank of England. The whole British police force will be after him!"

"He can escape abroad," said Jeremy Ralph, one of Mr. Fogg's companions. "He could travel to Egypt and vanish into the desert. Or slip into India or Hong Kong, and never be seen again."

"Not so easy today," interrupted Phileas Fogg. "The world has grown smaller with the coming of the steamships and railroads. I dare

"Where can the bank robber hide now?"

say you could travel right around the world in eighty days now. The robber will find it hard to escape detection wherever he goes."

"Eighty days! Never!" cried John Sullivan, another of his companions.

"I'd like to see you do it, Mr. Fogg," said Tom Flanagan, who was with the group.

Mr. Fogg looked Flanagan in the eye. "I'll do more than that. I shall wager you twenty thousand pounds that I can indeed travel around the world in eighty days."

"Twenty thousand pounds!" exclaimed Sullivan. "You could lose the bet by missing the last bus in Bombay. Or by traveling on a weary elephant in India, or being delayed at Oakland station in San Francisco!"

Phileas Fogg repeated the wager in very solemn and exact terms.

"I will bet twenty thousand pounds," he began, "that I can go around the world in eighty days or less. Do you accept my wager?"

Ralph, Sullivan, and Flanagan looked at each other for a moment. They answered as one. "Yes!"

"Very good," said Mr. Fogg. "The express train for the south coast leaves tonight at 8:45 p.m. I shall be on it. And that time will mark the start of the bet."

"I will bet twenty thousand pounds."

"What!" cried Ralph. "This very evening?"

"Indeed!" replied Phileas Fogg, taking out his diary.

He spent some time leafing through the months and days and then he spoke again. "Today is Wednesday, October 2, 1872. So to be back in eighty days means I shall see you here at the Reform Club at 8:45 p.m. on Saturday, December 21."

The three men were now looking at Phileas Fogg with some concern. It was not for fear of losing their money. They were good sports and wealthy men. No, they were sure it was a bet he could never win. The journey would be an extraordinarily dangerous one.

"Well, my friends," said Mr. Fogg, "it is now past seven o'clock and I must go home to prepare for my departure. So farewell for now. I shall see you either at the train station . . . or back here within eighty days."

Phileas Fogg rose from his chair, shook each man's hand, and left the room.

They all watched him go.

"My goodness!" said Ralph.

"My goodness indeed!" echoed Sullivan.

"By golly and gadzooks!" exclaimed Flanagan. "What an adventure! What a wager!"

Chapter 2
A Frenchman called Passepartout

Mr. Fogg arrived home from the Reform Club several hours earlier than expected.

His new French manservant, James Passepartout, was most surprised.

Passepartout had only been working for Mr. Fogg since 11:26 that morning; the exact time when he had been employed. Phileas Fogg was a very exact man. He was surprised at the early return because Mr. Fogg had told him that he never got home from the club until midnight.

"Passepartout, my good man," declared Phileas Fogg, as calmly as if he was asking for a cup of tea. "We're going around the world. We leave for France tonight."

A puzzled grin crept across Passepartout's face. "You are not leaving home are you, monsieur?" he asked.

"Not just me," said Mr. Fogg. "You and I are both leaving. We are going round the world. And we're going to do it in eighty days!"

Passepartout's eyes opened wide in astonishment. "Round the world, monsieur?" he murmured, almost too shocked to speak.

"Yes, around the world in eighty days," replied Mr. Fogg. "We haven't a moment to lose. Now we must get packed."

"But it will take me ages to pack!" protested Passepartout, who was a little lazy, it must be said. He had seen his new job as something that wouldn't involve too much hard work.

"One bag will be enough. My old green carpetbag will do," said Phileas Fogg urgently. "Two shirts, a pair of trousers, some underclothes, and three pairs of socks will do. The same for you. We'll buy more clothes on the way."

Passepartout, seeing all hopes of a quiet life quickly disappearing, went upstairs to pack.

Downstairs, Phileas Fogg pulled down a copy of Bradshaw's International Train and Steamship Timetable from a bookshelf. It was the guide to arrival and departure times of all the major steamships and trains around the world.

Passepartout returned shortly after, carrying

an ancient and dusty green carpetbag. It was a large bag with two leather straps for handles.

"I've packed all you asked for, monsieur," he said, putting the bag down.

Phileas Fogg went over to an old painting hanging on the wall of his study and took it down. Hidden behind it was a small safe. He turned the combination lock, opened the door, and removed a thick wad of English bank notes.

"Now put this in my bag," he said, handing the money to Passepartout. "Take good care of it. There's twenty thousand pounds there!"

"Yes, Mr. Fogg," said Passepartout, staring in amazement at the money.

Then the two men took their overcoats and hats, and left the house. They hailed a cab to the train station, arriving there at 8:30 p.m.

As they walked through the station entrance, Phileas Fogg saw a poor beggar woman lying in the gutter. He immediately put a hand into the carpetbag being carried by Passepartout and took out a twenty pound note. He gave it to the woman without a word.

The two men hurried to Platform One, to board the train to Dover, the harbor town where boats for France departed. Phileas Fogg was not surprised to see that his Reform Club

Passepartout is astonished

companions, Jeremy Ralph, John Sullivan, and Tom Flanagan, were there to see him off.

He pulled his passport from his pocket and showed it to the men. "You can examine my passport when I get back," he said, "and it will prove to you that I have gone around the world. It will be stamped at all the places I pass."

"That will be quite unnecessary," said Ralph. "We will trust the word of a gentleman."

"Don't forget when you are due back in London," said Sullivan.

"In eighty days," said Phileas Fogg, "on Saturday, December 21, at 8:45 p.m. Now gentlemen, we must be away."

Mr. Fogg and Passepartout, hanging onto the green carpetbag as if his life depended on it, seated themselves on the train at 8:40 p.m.

Five minutes later, the conductor's whistle blew. The locomotive roared and belched steam in all directions. The train started to move. In a moment, Phileas Fogg and Passepartout were thundering south into a dark, rain-filled night.

Passepartout looked at his master, who was now starting to slumber on the opposite seat.

Phileas Fogg was about forty years old, a few years older than Passepartout. He was tall, with fine handsome features, and light hair and

Putting the money into the bag

whiskers. But the most obvious thing about the man was his calmness. Passepartout wondered if anyone or anything could move or shake him.

Passepartout's mind went back to that morning when Mr. Fogg had given him a note with his duties written on it. It read:

> *Notes for the attention of my manservant.*
> *I am to be awakened at 8:00 each morning.*
> *Serve tea and toast in bed at 8:10 a.m.*
> *Shaving water to be heated by 8:25 a.m.*
> *Shaving water temperature to be exactly*
> *84 degrees Fahrenheit.*

Mr. Fogg had explained that his previous manservant had repeatedly served the water a degree too cold. That was why he had been forced to sack him from his post.

If Passepartout had been able to talk to Ralph, Sullivan, or Flanagan about Phileas Fogg, they could not have told him much about the man.

Mr. Fogg was something of a mystery to people. Certainly he was rich. But no one knew how he had made his fortune. He spoke little to anyone, and that made him even more mysterious. He had no real friends.

14

"Now gentlemen, we must be away."

Mr. Fogg's main occupation seemed to be to travel to the Reform Club each morning. There he read the newspapers or played cards with Ralph, Sullivan, and Flanagan.

He occasionally won money at cards, but he always gave away his winnings to charity. He breakfasted and dined at the Club, always at the same hour, always at the same table, and always alone.

Certainly, Phileas Fogg lived alone; a lonely man, some would have said.

***

Mr. Fogg had started to snore when the train roared into a tunnel. Suddenly, Passepartout let out a strangled cry of despair.

"What's the matter?" asked Mr. Fogg, waking with a start. "Has there been a murder?"

"No," replied Passepartout. "I've done something terrible. I was in such a hurry that I left the gas light burning in my room!"

Mr. Fogg smiled and said in his usual calm manner, "Well, we can't go back now. It will have to burn until we get home. And, of course, you will have to pay the account for your forgetfulness!"

Chapter 3
Detective Fix from Scotland Yard

Sitting in another part of the train was James Fix, a Scotland Yard detective. He was dreaming of catching the man who had so famously robbed the Bank of England of fifty-five thousand pounds.

Young and enthusiastic, Fix was a man on a mission—not to go around the world in eighty days, but to station himself at Port Suez in Egypt. There he would keep an eye open for the robber, should he try to escape by taking a boat to the mysterious East.

The robber had been seen leaving the Bank of England and police had issued a good description of the man. Fix had that description in his hand. He had spent hours studying the features of the wanted man.

Fix could already imagine the glory of returning to London with his man; not to mention the huge reward offered by the bank.

Even as the train rattled down to Dover,

there were only two topics of conversation back in London that night; the Bank of England robbery and Phileas Fogg's wager. News of the bet had spread fast.

The wager was all the talk in the Reform Club. Some members thought Mr. Fogg could win. Most shook their heads and said it would be impossible to go around the world in eighty days. No one had ever tried to do it before.

Most of the newspapers the next morning printed stories about the wager, saying that the journey was complete madness—an impossibility.

***

For several days, the Reform Club heard no word from Phileas Fogg. Then he sent news by telegraph wire that he had reached Italy by train and was about to board the Steamship *Mongolia* bound for Suez.

The *Mongolia* was due at Port Suez to load up with coal for the next section of its voyage. Then it would steam down the Suez Canal and across the Arabian Sea, to India, and the port of Bombay.

Mr. Fogg had shown Passepartout his diary,

Fix was a man on a mission.

in which he had planned out his journey around the world.

The short entry read:

Estimated journey times:
London-Suez, via Italy,   *. . . 7 days*
  by rail and boat
Suez-Bombay by steamship   *. . . 13 days*
Bombay-Calcutta (India)   *. . . 3 days*
  by rail
Calcutta-Hong Kong   *. . . 13 days*
  (British Colony)
  by steamship
Hong Kong-Yokohama   *. . . 6 days*
  (Japan) by steamship
Yokohama-San Francisco   *. . . 22 days*
  by steamship
San Francisco-New York   *. . . 7 days*
  by rail
New York-Liverpool   *. . . 8 days*
  (England) by steamship
Liverpool to London   *. . . 6 hours*
  by rail
            Total: 79 days and 6 hours

Even Passepartout realized that Phileas Fogg had not left much time for missed ships and trains, or other disasters on the way. But they were ahead of time so far. The *Mongolia* pulled into Port Suez early.

Detective Fix, who suffered dreadfully from seasickness, had spent most of the journey in his cabin. So there had been no chance for him to examine all the passengers.

Now, he was first off the ship and stood waiting at the bottom of the gangway, by which passengers reached the dockside. He studied each person leaving the ship.

At last Phileas Fogg, with Passepartout carrying the carpetbag, appeared at the top of the gangway. Fix could not believe his eyes as he stared at the two men. One of them looked exactly like the description he had of the bank robber.

The two travelers reached the dockside, where a member of the ship's crew spoke to them, saying, "Don't be late back, Mr. Fogg. We sail in four hours."

Detective Fix heard every word. "Fogg—a perfect name for a bank robber!" he thought to himself. He was sure he had found his man.

When the two men had disappeared down the road, Fix ordered the captain of the ship to show him the men's cabin. Phileas Fogg's diary lay open on the table. Fix read it with great interest.

Suez: I am still on time. Sail for India later today.

Fix was now certain he had his man. India! What a place for a robber to lie low without fear of being found. But there was a problem. He could not make an arrest without a special warrant from his Scotland Yard headquarters in England.

Fix hurried to the telegraph office, to send a message by telegraph wire all the way back to Scotland Yard in London.

The message said:

Am in Suez
I've found the bank robber; one Mr. Phileas Fogg. Please send warrant for his arrest without delay.
Detective Fix.

Fix didn't think it would take long for the warrant to be sent. In the meantime, he followed the direction that Mr. Fogg had taken.

By chance, Mr. Fogg and Passepartout had

He was sure he had found his man.

split up to go their separate ways. Phileas Fogg went to have his passport stamped at the Suez customs office, while Passepartout was doing some sightseeing.

Passepartout bumped into Fix as he was looking about. They started a conversation.

"So this is Suez?" asked Passepartout.

"Yes, it is," said Fix. "Surely you know where you are?"

"I seem to be traveling in a dream, monsieur," said Passepartout. "One moment I am in London, the next in Suez. It is Suez in Egypt, isn't it?"

"Yes," said Fix.

"Egypt in Africa?" asked Passepartout.

"In Africa," said Fix. "You do seem to be in a bit of a hurry."

"Not me," replied Passepartout. "But my master, Mr. Phileas Fogg, is."

"You left London in a hurry then?" said Fix, with a knowing smile.

"We certainly did."

"And where is your master going to?"

"Round the world," said Passepartout.

"Round the world!" cried Fix.

"Yes," said Passepartout, "Mr. Fogg has wagered some friends that he can travel around

"I seem to be traveling in a dream."

the world in eighty days. I don't see how he'll do it, myself. No man can go round the world in that time."

"This Mr. Fogg seems a bit of a character," said Fix, rubbing his nose suspiciously.

"I should say so, monsieur," answered Passepartout.

"Is he rich?" asked Fix, innocently.

"No doubt," said Passepartout. "He's carrying an enormous sum of money in bank notes with him. And he's very generous with it, too. He's promised the ship's captain a big reward if he gets us to Bombay ahead of time."

The already suspicious detective could hardly hide his excitement. Surely he had his bank robber. He was already imagining his glorious return to London with the villain in handcuffs!

Fix said a hasty goodbye to Passepartout and rushed back to the telegraph office. When he got there, he found that the arrest warrant had not arrived. And the *Mongolia*, with Mr. Fogg and Passepartout on it, was about to leave.

Fix realized he would have to travel on to India, or let his man escape. He could just as well arrest Mr. Fogg in Bombay. Besides he had never been to India. It would make a nice trip.

He told the local police chief in Suez to forward the warrant to Bombay when it arrived.

Then he bought a ticket and hurried aboard.

Chapter 4
To India by Steamship!

The *Mongolia* steamed down the Red Sea from Suez, a burning hot wind blowing in from the desert and across the tops of the ancient pyramids.

While Fix had retired to his cabin with sea-sickness again, Phileas Fogg and Passepartout had no trouble with the tossing sea.

On the first day that Fix felt well enough to have a walk on deck, he bumped into Passepartout again.

"Well, what a surprise!" said Passepartout, on seeing Fix.

"Oh, you're the servant of that strange Englishman," said Fix, innocently.

"Indeed," said Passepartout. "And where are you bound?"

"Like you, I'm going to Bombay, or even farther. I haven't made up my mind yet," answered Fix. "And how is Mr. Fogg? I haven't seen him on deck at all."

"Well, what a surprise!"

"You won't, monsieur," said Passepartout. "He doesn't like fresh air. He stays below, playing cards and reading."

Fix looked suspicious. "You know," he said, "one might think Mr. Fogg was on some special mission and didn't want to be observed in what he was up to."

"Oh, I don't think so," said Passepartout. "Even if he is up to something, I know nothing about it. Neither do I care to find out."

After this first meeting on the ship, Passepartout and Fix met regularly. Each time, Fix became more and more convinced of one thing; if Mr. Fogg was the bank robber, then Passepartout knew nothing about what his master had been up to.

Aden, 1,310 miles from Suez and located at the southern extreme of the Red Sea, was the next stop. The *Mongolia* had to take on more coal. The ship arrived fifteen hours ahead of schedule and, once more, Phileas Fogg went ashore to have his passport stamped.

That evening the ship set off again on the 1,650 mile leg of the journey to Bombay.

The *Mongolia* made good time across the Gulf of Arabia and soon the coast of India came in sight. At 4:30 p.m. on Sunday,

October 20, the ship arrived in Bombay—two days early.

Phileas Fogg was delighted with his progress. His first glance through his cabin porthole at Bombay made him smile, too. He saw one of the ship's passengers running down the gangway to the dockside. The man, who he had never seen in his life before, was going so fast that he stumbled and fell.

Detective Fix was in a hurry. He picked himself up and raced off to the local police station to see if the warrant for Mr. Fogg's arrest had arrived. It hadn't.

Fix was annoyed beyond words. But at least he had learned from Passepartout that Phileas Fogg's next journey would be by rail to Calcutta, on the opposite side of the country. Once more, Fix asked for the warrant to be sent on, this time to Calcutta.

Early that evening, the train steamed off on the journey to Calcutta with Mr. Fogg and Passepartout—and Fix—aboard.

The green bag was looking a little fuller than usual. In Bombay, Passepartout had bought himself a present to show his friends back home. It was the costume of an Indian Rajah, or Prince.

The costume included a turban headdress, a white cotton robe, and a pair of colorful Indian slippers covered in false pearls. Passepartout was sure he would look every inch an Indian Rajah in those clothes when he got back to England!

Several hours after the journey began, Phileas Fogg retired to their sleeping cabin. Passepartout decided to explore the train. As he wandered into the dining car, he was a trifle surprised to find Fix on board.

"We meet again, my friend!" he said.

"I thought I'd go on to Calcutta," explained the detective. "It will be an interesting journey, and I've nothing better to do."

Passepartout had never been bold enough to ask Fix what he did for a living. He wondered if he was a wealthy man, traveling for his own enjoyment. With a wave goodnight, he returned to the sleeping cabin.

To Passepartout, the whole trip seemed incredible. One moment he had been starting a new job in London; now he was crossing India in a steam train.

He was amazed at the changing landscape. From the train window, he saw flat plains, then mountains, hills, and thick jungle.

One thing he couldn't quite understand was

He was going so fast that he stumbled and fell.

how the time, as related to London, changed the farther east they traveled. They seemed to be gaining time minute by minute.

Passepartout owned a beautiful old watch that was a family heirloom. It was at least one hundred years old. He was very proud of it and wore it at all times.

Earlier that evening, Phileas Fogg had asked him what the time and date was.

Passepartout took a look at his watch. "Exactly 10:00 p.m. on October 20, monsieur," he said.

"I don't think so," smiled Phileas Fogg. "It is indeed 10:00 p.m. in London, but it is now four hours earlier than that by Indian time. Where we are right now, it is only 6:00 p.m."

"Of course, I'm sure you are right," apologized Passepartout. "But I have decided to keep my watch running on London time."

Mr. Fogg smiled. He was quite happy for his servant to stay on London time, if he preferred to do so!

The next day the train came to a sudden halt, just fifty miles short of Allahabad in central India.

"Why has the train stopped?" Phileas Fogg asked the conductor.

The whole trip seemed incredible

"There is no rail line between here and Allahabad," he explained. "It hasn't been built yet."

"But the newspapers said the line had been opened," protested Mr. Fogg.

"You mustn't believe everything you read in newspapers, good sir," said the conductor. "Passengers have to find their own way from here to Allahabad."

Phileas Fogg remained calm. He was in no hurry; he was still at least two days ahead of schedule. His next target was October 25, when a steamship left Calcutta for Hong Kong.

It was Passepartout who came up with an idea how to get to Allahabad.

"When in India, travel like the Indian," he said to his master.

Phileas Fogg was confused.

"An elephant, monsieur," cried Passepartout. "We must travel by elephant!"

Chapter 5
An Elephant Ride to Allahabad

"An elephant!" cried Phileas Fogg. "A wonderful idea, Passepartout!"

It didn't take them long to find a local man who had an elephant for sale; a lovely creature called Kiouni.

"But how will we find an elephant driver?" asked Mr. Fogg.

"I can ride an elephant," said Passepartout. "I did not tell you before, monsieur, but in one of my many jobs I worked in a circus in Paris. There, I learned to handle elephants."

"Passepartout, you're a clever old devil!" cried Mr. Fogg.

It was only the first of many surprises that Passepartout would give his master on their journey.

The elephant came with a box-like saddle called a *howdah* on its back. There was room for two people to sit in it.

With Kiouni on her knees, Phileas Fogg

"I can ride an elephant."

clambered aboard. Then Passepartout climbed into the driver's position on Kiouni's neck. A gentle tap with a stick was enough to get the elephant to her feet and walking forward.

They hadn't gone far when Passepartout suddenly saw Fix. He was some distance ahead on the same road.

Fix was finding his own way to Allahabad on a "bone-shaker", a new type of bicycle with one large wheel at the front, a small wheel at the back, and a seat between them. The detective didn't see a laughing Passepartout aboard the elephant as he bumped and rattled on his way.

Passepartout had not mentioned Fix to his master, nor had he any intention of doing so. It was not something Phileas Fogg would be interested in.

Yet, Passepartout was becoming a little intrigued with this fellow traveler. He had begun to suspect that Fix was something more than just a wealthy man, wandering the world . . .

Kiouni proved to be quite a speedy animal when she was trotting. But travel at that pace proved very uncomfortable, and her passengers were bumped and jolted about.

In the middle of the day, with the sun burning fiercely on their necks, they stopped to rest in a small village. There, they heard a terrible story about a young Indian girl called Aouda.

Aouda had been promised in marriage to an old man more than twice her age. But the girl, they were told, would have rather died than marry him. So she had run away and no one had seen her for weeks.

Mr. Fogg was horrified when he heard this. He felt so sorry for Aouda, imagining her all alone with no one to turn to. "We must forget our journey and help find her," he decided. "A girl's life is more important than any bet!"

Passepartout knew that his master was a

Fix was riding a bone-shaker.

40

generous man. So he wasn't surprised at all that he was prepared to risk losing the twenty thousand pound bet to help a total stranger.

Mr. Fogg talked to several people in the village and they thought that the girl would probably be traveling in the direction of Allahabad. It was a big town, they said. Aouda could certainly hide away there.

The next morning, Phileas Fogg and Passepartout set off aboard Kiouni, determined to find the poor girl.

They saw no sign of Aouda on the road that day. But when they stopped for the night, they spotted a campfire burning in a forest clearing not far off. They decided to investigate.

Tying Kiouni to a tree, they slowly crept toward the camp. Now they could hear voices and see shadows moving about.

The night was so dark that they managed to get to within a few yards of the camp without raising the alarm. They saw six men sitting around a fire. Each man had a musket beside him.

Tied to a tree close by, was the most beautiful girl Phileas Fogg had ever seen.

She looked to be about twenty years old, and she was sobbing pitifully. It had to be Aouda.

"We can't take on six armed men," whispered Mr. Fogg. "Any ideas, Passepartout?"

Some people might have thought that Passepartout was a simple man, even foolish at times. But he had a very imaginative brain.

"I certainly do, monsieur," he grinned.

***

A few hours later, at the dead of night, the six armed men were awoken by the sound of something heavy approaching through the undergrowth.

They heard a chilling cry from some mysterious jungle beast. The sounds came closer and closer.

The men saw what appeared to be an elephant, although it was too dark to tell, really. And sitting on top of the beast was someone, or something, making a terrible moaning sound.

The creature emerged from the shadows and the men could hardly believe their eyes. Now they could see that it definitely was an elephant, and it was being ridden by the ghostly apparition of an Indian prince!

His face was ashen white. He was wearing a white turban, a long white robe that covered

A ghostly apparition

him from head to toe, and shoes that glittered like diamonds in the reflection of the fire.

The six men stared in horror at this strange appearance. Whether or not they believed the figure to be the ghost of some long dead Indian prince will never be known.

Jumping to their feet, the men raced away, terror stricken and screaming, into the forest.

Chapter 6
Aouda's story

The Indian girl was just as terrified when the ghostly prince approached her.

"Who are you?" she cried, expecting to be murdered at any minute.

"A friend," said Passepartout, starting to gently untie the ropes that bound her. "You must be Aouda. We've been looking for you. You are safe now."

Passepartout led the girl over to his master, who was hurrying towards them. She smiled when she saw the kindly face of Phileas Fogg.

Mr. Fogg slapped Passepartout on the back to congratulate him. "Where have the men gone?" he asked.

"They ran for their lives after seeing me dressed up like a ghostly Indian prince with chalk dust on my face," Passepartout replied.

"What would I do without you," said Phileas Fogg.

Aouda told her story that night. She was the

daughter of a rich Bombay merchant, who had become an orphan when she lost her parents as a young girl. She had been cared for in an orphanage by a British nanny. That's why she spoke such good English.

Aouda was still living at the orphanage when an old friend of her late father arrived. He said that her father had promised Aouda in marriage to him.

"There was nothing I could do," said Aouda. "It was either obey this man or run away. I chose to run away. And that's when I was captured by the six men you saw. They were taking me to Allahabad to be sold into slavery."

Phileas Fogg felt so sorry for the girl. "So where will you go now?" he asked.

"I have no one to turn to," she said sadly, "except for a cousin who lives in Hong Kong. I believe he's wealthy and would look after me."

"That settles it then," said a delighted Mr. Fogg. "We're going to Hong Kong. You will come with us!"

***

The next evening, the little group reached Allahabad. For Passepartout, it was time to say

"Who are you?"

goodbye to Kiouni. He was so sad when Phileas Fogg sold her to a kindly elephant driver, who would take her back to his village. He gave her a handful of sugar lumps before she trotted off with her new master.

Mr. Fogg did some calculations. He estimated it would take another twenty-four hours by rail from Allahabad to Calcutta. That would allow plenty of time for them to catch the steamer for Hong Kong.

Soon after, Phileas Fogg, Passepartout, and Aouda were aboard a comfortable train, racing across a glorious land populated by wild tigers, bears, and wolves.

As dawn crept over the horizon the next morning, the train roared into the valley of the Ganges, the most sacred river in India. It traveled all day and reached Calcutta at 7:00 p.m. on October 25, with five hours to spare before the steamer left.

Phileas Fogg had his passport stamped and went off with Passepartout and Aouda to see the city.

Detective Fix had also reached Calcutta by train. He was still suffering the agonies of his bumpy bicycle ride to Allahabad, and was in a very bad mood.

Saying goodbye to Kiouni

Fix's first task on arriving in Calcutta was to hurry to the main police station to see if the warrant for Mr. Fogg's arrest had arrived. He was furious when he discovered once more that he was still ahead of the warrant.

Fix checked with the local shipping office and learned that Phileas Fogg was booked on the steamship *Rangoon* that afternoon, for the voyage to Hong Kong.

There was only one thing he could do. And that was to buy a ticket for Hong Kong

Buying a ticket for Hong Kong

himself. Before leaving, he sent another telegraph message to Scotland Yard.

Am in Calcutta.
Warrant for the arrest of Mr. Phileas Fogg has
still not arrived. Please forward it immediately
to Hong Kong police headquarters.
Detective Fix

Fix boarded the *Rangoon* and quickly went and hid in his cabin. He didn't want to be seen because he just wanted to observe Phileas Fogg for a while.

He was peering out of his porthole window when Mr. Fogg, Passepartout, and Aouda arrived at the boat.

"The rascal's off again," he said to himself, "but I shall follow him to the end of the world if necessary. If he didn't commit the bank robbery, then my name's mud."

It was then that he realized that Mr. Fogg and Passepartout were not alone. The woman in between them was obviously traveling in their party.

A flurry of ideas fluttered through Fix's mind. Was this woman Mr. Fogg's accomplice? Or were all three of them in on the robbery?

There was another thing worrying Detective Fix at that moment. He had seen how much money Phileas Fogg had been spending.

What, with all the new clothes, ship and train tickets, and everything else, the man must have spent five thousand pounds of the proceeds from the robbery already!

Fix knew that the more Phileas Fogg spent, the less would be recovered when he arrested him. The detective saw his reward bounty getting smaller and smaller.

"Blast the man!" he cursed. "I must arrest him soon or else there'll be no reward left at all."

Yet it wasn't just the money. Fix was looking forward to the glory and fame of catching the most famous bank robber of the age.

Chapter 7
Fix Fails Again

The distance from Calcutta to Hong Kong was some 3,500 miles. Phileas Fogg hoped he could complete the journey in record time on the steamship *Rangoon*. She was a very fast vessel.

Steaming across the Bay of Bengal, heading south, Aouda spent much of her time learning to play cards with Mr. Fogg in his cabin. They passed the time very pleasantly—unlike Detective Fix.

Fix sat alone in his cabin, worrying. He had only intended going as far as Suez in his hunt for the great bank robber. And now here he was on his way to Hong Kong, on the other side of the world.

He didn't believe in the wager at all. To him, it was just a cover for a very clever bank robber called Phileas Fogg. He was sure that sooner or later, Mr. Fogg intended to vanish with what remained of the money.

Would Mr. Fogg make a run for it in Hong

Kong? Or Japan? Or America? And who would go with him? Passepartout? The strange new woman? Or both?

Fix's head was full of doubts. "I failed to catch my man in Suez," he thought. "He got away in Bombay and Calcutta. I must not fail in Hong Kong!" He decided it was time to have another talk with Passepartout.

"My goodness!" cried Passepartout, when he saw Fix appear on deck. "You! Here! What a surprise! I thought we left you in India. Are you going round the world too?"

"No. No," answered Fix. "I suddenly decided to travel on to Hong Kong. I have some business to attend to there."

"But how is it I haven't seen you on deck since Calcutta?" asked Passepartout. "You haven't been hiding from us, have you?"

"I was suffering rather badly from seasickness," Fix replied. "The seas in the Bay of Bengal don't agree with me."

Fix quickly changed the subject. "And how is Mr. Fogg?" he asked.

"As well and as punctual as ever," said Passepartout. "He's not a day behind time. He is so precise in his plans to circle the world and win his bet."

They passed the time very pleasantly.

"And his good lady," continued Fix, "I haven't had the chance of meeting her yet."

"She is well," said Passepartout, determined not to let this inquisitive man know everything about his master's life.

Passepartout was beginning to feel very suspicious of Fix. Was it just by chance that the man kept reappearing in their lives? The further they traveled, the surer Passepartout was that he was following them.

"I thought we left you in India."

Passepartout had become very fond of his master. He saw it as his job to protect him from any mischief. And what mischief was Fix up to?

Suddenly, he hit on an idea. Perhaps the man was an agent for those from the Reform Club who had taken the bet with Mr. Fogg; maybe Fix was a spy sent to keep an eye on Phileas Fogg and make sure he didn't cheat.

"Phileas Fogg, a cheat? Nothing could be farther from the truth," thought Passepartout. "Mr. Fogg is a most honorable gentleman!"

The more he thought about the idea, the more Passepartout became convinced his theory was correct. He now saw Fix in a very different light.

But he decided to say nothing to his master. He couldn't be absolutely sure he was right. And besides, Phileas Fogg would find it very hard to believe that his Club companions mistrusted him so much.

Chapter 8
Sightseeing in Singapore

On Wednesday, October 30, the *Rangoon* stopped off at Singapore, on its way to Hong Kong. Phileas Fogg consulted his notebook and was pleased to see that the journey from Calcutta to Singapore had taken half a day less than expected. To celebrate, he took Aouda for a sightseeing tour of Singapore in a horse-drawn carriage.

Mr. Fogg was not aware that Fix had called up another carriage and was following him as closely as he dared. What Fix didn't know was that someone was following *him*, too! The loyal Passepartout had taken yet another carriage.

Passepartout couldn't help but smile as he watched Fix follow his master about for the next two hours. At one time the three carriages were all parked—a good distance from each other—outside the customs office, while Phileas Fogg had his passport stamped.

The convoy of carriages returned to the ship

A sightseeing tour of Singapore

and at 11:00 the next morning, the *Rangoon* steamed out of Singapore into the South China Sea, on its way to Hong Kong.

The weather, which had been fine for most of the journey, suddenly took a turn for the worse. The wind rose and the seas began to roll. A storm was blowing up.

Phileas Fogg did not worry. The wind was blowing from the south and that would only add speed to the ship.

Their speed cheered up Passepartout too, who often reminded himself that his gaslight was still burning away in London. The sooner he got back to London, the less it would cost him.

Fix, poor fellow, was not a happy man. Monsieur Passepartout had started to wink at him now and again. What sort of wink was it? A sort of knowing wink? The sort of wink that made Fix think Passepartout knew something special about him.

And Passepartout did—or at least he thought he did. He was convinced that Fix was in the pay of the men from the Reform Club. His wink was a way of telling Fix that he knew what he was up to, and a warning to watch his step.

Fix, of course, took the wink a very different

What sort of wink was it?

way. He was now wondering if Passepartout suspected him of being a policeman.

"Mr. Fix," said Passepartout, knowing full well the answer to his question, "will you be traveling on with us after Hong Kong?"

"I don't know," he said, hesitantly. "I might. Perhaps. Perhaps not."

"There's not much point in going back now," Passepartout pointed out. "The next stop after Hong Kong will be Japan, and then America. And from America, England is but a step away."

"I'll have to think about it," said Fix. "You must understand that I don't travel at my own expense. I am paid for this journey."

"Oh, I'm quite sure of that," chuckled Passepartout, with another knowing wink.

That wink was beginning to infuriate Detective Fix!

Chapter 9
Hong Kong

The *Rangoon* steamed on towards Hong Kong, heading into a stormy gale. The farther she went, the more confused Fix and Passepartout became about each other.

Passepartout was convinced that Fix was a spy for the gentlemen of the Reform Club, although he still wouldn't tell his master until he had proof. He had no idea at all that Fix was a detective.

Fix was now sure that Passepartout suspected him of being a detective, and was desperately worried that he would tell Phileas Fogg. If he did, Mr. Fogg might immediately make a run for it.

Passepartout's wink was confusing Fix, too. What part was the Frenchman playing in all of this? Was he, or was he not, an accomplice to that robbery at the Bank of England?

And what of Aouda? Who was she? However much he pressed Passepartout for information, the only answers he got were so vague that they gave him no clue at all. Even so, he was still fairly sure that Passepartout was an honest man and knew nothing about the robbery.

Fix desperately hoped that Passepartout wouldn't tell Mr. Fogg he was a detective. With luck, the arrest warrant would be in Hong Kong when they arrived and he would finally get his man.

Meanwhile, below deck, Phileas Fogg was blissfully unaware of any of this. He was looking

Heading into a stormy gale

forward to reaching Hong Kong, but there was one other thing on his mind; losing Aouda. Hong Kong was where she was hoping to meet her cousin.

Phileas Fogg and Aouda were spending long hours together now, playing cards or just talking. They had become quite fond of each other — not that Phileas Fogg would have recognized Aouda's affection for him.

So the *Rangoon* rolled northwards into the gale. They were now starting to lose time. Mr. Fogg gazed out of his cabin porthole and did his calculations. He estimated that they would reach Hong Kong some twenty hours behind schedule.

That still left him plenty of time to catch the steamship *Carnatic*, which was due to carry him from Hong Kong to Yokohama, in Japan. He hadn't even thought about missing the boat yet. To Phileas Fogg, there was no such thing as failure.

As for Passepartout, he was very anxious about the weather. He kept bothering the crew with questions about how long the gale would last, and how long they thought it would take to reach Hong Kong.

The twenty thousand pound bet was not his

to win, but he had come to see himself as part of the success of that wager. He dearly wanted Phileas Fogg to be the victor.

The storm finally blew itself out and the ship reached Hong Kong on the morning of November 6, at exactly 5:00 a.m.

Passepartout was very distressed. Five o'clock in the morning was the very moment the Steamship *Carnatic* was due to leave Hong Kong for Yokohama. There was no way they could catch that ship now. The bet would be lost!

Phileas Fogg, Passepartout, and Aouda — closely followed by Fix skulking after them — went ashore and asked an official whether the *Carnatic* had actually left on time.

"Oh, no, sir," replied the man. "She didn't leave this morning. They are still mending one of her boilers. She won't sail until nine o'clock tomorrow morning."

Passepartout jumped into the air with delight. Fix scowled and hurried off to the police station, to see if the arrest warrant had arrived.

He returned minutes later with an even angrier expression on his face. The warrant had still not appeared. He had been told it might be another three days before it arrived because the main telegraph lines were all down.

He jumped into the air with delight.

Later that morning, Phileas Fogg, Passepartout, and Aouda took a carriage into town. Only the Frenchman noticed Fix's long shadow following them.

The first thing they did was to try and find Aouda's relation. The news was bad. Her cousin had died the year before.

"What shall I do now?" cried Aouda, turning to her friend, Phileas Fogg.

"It is very simple," replied the kind gentleman. "You must travel on with us to England."

There was nothing left for Aouda in India. And now, there was no reason for her to stay in Hong Kong. There was nothing to prevent her from traveling to England.

Phileas Fogg took the carpetbag from Passepartout, explaining that he wanted to buy a few things that morning. Then he gave his servant some money to buy a ship's ticket for Aouda.

Passepartout was very pleased Aouda was coming with them, and went off to book another ticket on the *Carnatic*. When he reached the ship, he saw that Fix had followed him.

"Well, Mr. Fix," said Passepartout, knowingly, "have you decided to go on with us as far as Japan and America?"

"What shall I do now?"

"Possibly, Monsieur Passepartout," answered Fix. "We shall see. It may not be necessary."

"I suspect you will be coming along with us," said Passepartout, with another knowing wink. "I don't think you can bear to be parted from us."

The news from the ticket office made Fix even less happy. The *Carnatic*'s repairs had been completed early and she was now due to leave that evening, rather than early the next day.

Passepartout was delighted. It would put his master almost on time again.

Fix, on the other hand, was desperate. He knew he now had to make a move, or risk losing his man for good.

Chapter 10
Tricked!

Fix now decided to take Passepartout into his confidence and tell him all. It seemed the only way he could possibly keep Phileas Fogg in Hong Kong until the arrest warrant arrived.

"Passepartout," he said, "it's time we went for a drink and a talk. There's plenty of time to tell Mr. Fogg that the ship is leaving earlier than expected."

"Very well," winked Passepartout, "perhaps you have a little secret to reveal to me."

"How did you know?" asked Fix.

"Just a guess, Mr. Fix," replied Passepartout.

They found a hotel and sat down in a room to talk. Passepartout had never drunk a drop of alcohol in his life before, but Fix ordered a bottle of whisky and poured out two glasses.

What followed was a very strange conversation. The two men were talking together, yet they were discussing two completely different things.

Fix put his hand on Passepartout's arm and, lowering his voice, whispered, "You have guessed who I am, I believe."

Passepartout nodded knowingly and took a sip of whisky. He winced at the sharp taste.

Fix continued. "Then I'm going to tell you everything . . ."

"Perhaps I know everything already," said Passepartout, "and all I will say is that those gentlemen who have employed you to follow my master have wasted a great deal of money on you. My master would never cheat them."

The answer completely confused Fix. "What on earth are you talking about?" he asked.

"A matter of twenty thousand pounds!" said Passepartout.

"It's not twenty thousand pounds," declared Fix. "It's a matter of fifty-five thousand pounds."

"My goodness!" said Passepartout. "I thought the bet was twenty thousand pounds but if it is truly fifty-five thousand pounds, then there's all the more reason for us to hurry on to Yokohama. We mustn't be late!"

Fix suddenly realized that the two of them were talking about different things.

"Look here," he said. "Just who do you think I am?"

They found a hotel.

"It's been obvious to me for some time now," said Passepartout. "You have been employed as a spy by members of the Reform Club. Your job is to see Monsieur Fogg doesn't cheat!"

Fix looked quite shocked, as Passepartout continued.

"Although I know that you were the agent for these faithless men, I have taken good care to say nothing about it to Mr. Fogg."

"He knows nothing, then?" asked Fix, anxiously.

"Nothing!" said Passepartout, emptying his glass.

"Excellent!" replied Fix, pouring Passepartout a second drink. "Now I must tell you that I am not, as you seem to think, an agent of the members of the Reform Club."

"Bah!" cried Passepartout.

"I am an English police detective sent out from London . . ."

"You, a detective?" interrupted Passepartout.

"I can prove it," said Fix, pulling his identification card from a pocket.

Passepartout looked at the card in amazement. There was no doubting it. Fix was a Scotland Yard detective.

"Listen," continued Fix. "On September 28,

Fix was a Scotland Yard detective.

a robbery took place at the Bank of England. Fifty-five thousand pounds was stolen. Fortunately we have a good description of the robber, and it fits Mr. Phileas Fogg exactly."

"My master is the most honest of men!" exclaimed Passepartout.

"How can you tell?" demanded Fix. "From what you have told me, you scarcely know anything about him. You only joined him as his manservant on the day you left London."

"He is an honest man. I am sure of it!" insisted Passepartout, losing a little of his confidence.

"You could be arrested as his accomplice," said Fix, with a threatening look in his eye. "You could spend years in prison."

Passepartout didn't know what to think.

"What do you want of me?" he asked, at last.

"I have yet to receive a warrant for Mr. Fogg's arrest from England," said Fix. "It will come within a day or so. All I want you to do is to help me keep him here in Hong Kong until it arrives."

Passepartout was shocked. How could he be involved in a plot to keep his master in Hong Kong? It would destroy any hopes of Mr. Fogg winning the bet.

Tricked!

Fix wasn't finished. "I will share with you the reward offered by the Bank of England," he said. "The amount stolen was fifty-five thousand pounds and I believe much of that is still in the carpetbag that you usually carry for him. I will get a large share of that as my reward for catching the culprit. If you help me, you can have five hundred pounds."

"I will not help a scoundrel like you for all the money in the world!" cried Passepartout.

The whisky then started to go to his head, and he began to feel a fuzziness come over him.

"You refuse to help me then?" said Fix sternly.

"Certainly," mumbled Passepartout. "Whatever the truth of the matter, I am still Mr. Phileas Fogg's servant. I have seen his generosity and goodness, and I will never betray him."

Fix suddenly became thoughtful. "In that case," he said at last, "it is my duty as a policeman to order that you say nothing to anyone — especially Mr. Fogg — about what I have told you today. Forget every word!"

"Why should I?" said Passepartout, his blurry eyes blinking open and shut.

Loyal Passepartout was close to dozing off from the effects of the drink.

"*You refuse to help me then?*"

"Dear Mr. Passepartout," said Fix, quietly, "one more drink with an old friend, eh?"

Passepartout took one sip. "I am not your friend!" he mumbled.

Those were the last words he said before slumping back in his chair, his head on his chest. He had fallen deeply asleep.

Fix smiled as he looked down at the unconscious Passepartout. "When Passepartout wakes up, the *Carnatic* will have gone," he muttered under his breath. "And with luck, Phileas Fogg will not have realized that the ship left early. He'll be stuck in Hong Kong until the warrant for his arrest arrives!"

Fix paid the account and left Passepartout asleep in his chair.

Chapter 11
Passepartout Vanishes

Phileas Fogg had been a little surprised when Passepartout did not return to the hotel that night. He had gone to bed assuming that his manservant would turn up later, but in the morning there was still no sign of him.

Guessing that Passepartout had left early to prepare the cabins in the *Carnatic*, he and Aouda made their way down to the harbor. The *Carnatic* was nowhere to be seen.

When Phileas Fogg discovered that the *Carnatic* had sailed, he remained quite calm. He was more concerned for Passepartout's safety than missing the boat.

"Never mind the boat," he said to Aouda, "we must find Passepartout."

"What if Passepartout is on the *Carnatic*?" wondered Aouda.

"If he's on the boat we'll eventually catch up with him," said Phileas Fogg. "If he's here in Hong Kong, we'll find him."

The Carnatic was nowhere to be seen.

Just then, a man who had been observing Phileas Fogg closely made his approach. It was, of course, Detective Fix.

"Excuse me, sir," he said, "but I couldn't help overhearing you."

"Sorry," said Phileas Fogg, "I don't think we have met before."

"We haven't, sir," replied Fix, "but I got to know your servant Passepartout quite well on the journey out."

"Do you know where he is?" asked Aouda anxiously.

"Isn't he with you?" said Fix, pretending to be surprised.

"No," said Aouda. "Could he have sailed on the *Carnatic* without us?"

"I have no idea. Did you intend to sail on the *Carnatic*?" replied Fix, as if he didn't know the answer.

Phileas Fogg and Aouda replied that they were booked to sail on her.

"So was I," said Fix. "It was such a shame to find the ship had gone earlier than expected."

"The next steamship is due in a week, I believe," said Phileas Fogg quietly.

"So you'll be staying here for a few days,

then," said Fix, who was sure the warrant would arrive well before the next ship.

"Maybe, maybe not," said Mr. Fogg. "There seems to be plenty of other vessels in the harbor. Come on, Aouda, let's see if we can find another boat to take us."

They walked off with Fix following, as if linked by an invisible thread.

For three hours they wandered around the harbor trying to find someone to take them on to Yokohama.

Phileas Fogg was about to give up when a sailor called across to him, "John Bunsby, captain of the *Tankadere* at your service. Are you looking for a boat, sir?"

"I am," said Mr. Fogg cheerfully.

The man led them across to his boat. "Is my boat good enough for you, sir?" asked Captain Bunsby.

"Will she get me all the way to Yokohama?" asked Mr. Fogg.

"Yokohama! You must be joking," replied Captain Bunsby. There was no way his little boat could handle the heavy seas they might encounter on the way.

"I am not joking," said Phileas Fogg firmly. "I have to get to Yokohama by the fourteenth day of this month, to catch a ship to San Francisco."

"I'm sorry, sir," apologized the man. "It would be impossible in this small boat."

Mr. Fogg immediately offered the man two hundred pounds a day for the journey and a bonus of another two hundred pounds if they reached Yokohama on time.

The captain went off to discuss the offer with his crew. He returned a few minutes later.

"It would be impossible for me to reach Yokohama," explained the captain. "But I do have another suggestion. I could get you to Shanghai, which is only eight hundred miles from here."

"What's the use of Shanghai," said Phileas Fogg, "when I have to get to Yokohama?"

The captain explained. "If you look again in your timetable you will see that the steamship that sails from Yokohama on November 14 begins its voyage a few days earlier in Shanghai."

"My goodness, so it does!" said Phileas Fogg, thumbing through his book of timetables.

The captain continued. "The boat leaves Shanghai on November 11. It's only November 7 now, so we have four days. With good luck and a good wind we could make it in time."

"Are you looking for a boat, sir?"

Phileas Fogg put down his carpetbag, opened it and counted out two hundred pounds in banknotes. He gave the money to Bunsby.

"Right, get your boat ready for noon," said Phileas Fogg. "I have some business to attend to here first."

"My boat and crew will be ready for you, sir," replied the captain.

"Mr. Fix," said Phileas Fogg, seeing the man lurking close by, "why don't you come with us?"

Fix was absolutely terrified of boarding the small boat for such a long and dangerous journey. But he had no choice. Phileas Fogg must be kept in sight.

In the next few hours before the boat sailed, Phileas Fogg and Aouda combed the city, looking for Passepartout. They found no sign of him. Finally, they went to the local police station.

They gave police the description of Passepartout and left one thousand pounds, for a search to be mounted for the Frenchman.

"When you find him, tell him to book a ship back to England," said Phileas Fogg, handing over another three hundred pounds. "And remind him to turn off his gaslight when he gets there!"

Looking for Passepartout

With that, Mr. Fogg and Aouda returned to Captain Bunsby's boat, the *Tankadere*. It was a small, graceful two-masted sailing vessel of twenty tons. The decks and the brass work gleamed in the sunshine. Captain Bunsby obviously took great pride in his boat. He had a crew of four hardy seamen.

Phileas Fogg and Aouda went aboard, and found that Fix had already settled into one of the cabins. Fix was in an excellent mood. There was no sign of Passepartout, so his secret was safe for now.

The captain ordered the sails to be raised and the *Tankadere* slipped out of Hong Kong into the South China Sea, at noon on November 7.

Neither Phileas Fogg nor Aouda slept a wink that night for worrying about their dear friend, Passepartout.

Chapter 12
Bound for Shanghai

The eight hundred mile voyage to Shanghai was a perilous one for such a boat as the *Tankadere.* The seas around China at that time of year were very stormy.

Phileas Fogg reminded the captain that he must go as fast as possible, whatever the weather.

"Trust me, Mr. Fogg," was the reply. "I shall be raising as much sail as I can without risking losing my masts."

"I have the utmost confidence in you," answered Phileas Fogg.

As the sun set that night, Mr. Fogg stood proudly, legs wide apart, at the front of the boat. It was as if he was riding the waves.

Aouda stood behind him, staring out on the wide ocean. Above her, the wind-filled sails drove the boat forward.

Fix was sitting at the back of the boat, keeping himself apart from the other travelers. He was feeling terribly seasick.

At sunrise the following day, November 8, the boat had traveled more than one hundred miles. The *Tankadere* was racing ahead with all sails flying.

By evening, the boat entered the narrow storm-tossed Strait of Formosa.

Captain Bunsby looked at the cloudy skies ahead. "There's a huge storm coming," he warned.

Phileas Fogg looked calmly towards the ever-darkening skies. "Tell me, Captain," he said, "when the storm hits will the wind be behind us, or against us?"

"It'll be behind us," replied Captain Bunsby.

"If that's the case," said Phileas Fogg, "then it will carry us forward a little faster. So there will be no need to reduce speed."

The captain knew there was no point in arguing with Phileas Fogg, however great the danger ahead. So he kept the boat moving under full sail.

When the violent storm hit, the *Tankadere* was lifted like a feather by the wind and blown forward at a great rate of knots, perhaps moving faster than a train.

The boat raced north on huge waves all day long. Sometimes it plunged into deep watery

It was as if he was riding the waves.

valleys and looked as though it might capsize. But somehow, the *Tankadere* always found a way out again.

The passengers were continually bathed in spray. Fix sat at the back of the ship, almost frozen with fear and seasickness. Aouda stood close to Phileas Fogg, always trusting in his luck. Mr. Fogg himself just looked out on the storm as if it was an everyday event!

As the night came on, the storm increased. It became so violent that Captain Bunsby warned Mr. Fogg that it was time to seek shelter in one of the coastal ports.

"I agree entirely," answered Phileas Fogg.

"But which port?" asked the captain.

"I know only of one," smiled Mr. Fogg, "Shanghai!"

Captain Bunsby was about to say Shanghai was their final destination when he realized that Phileas Fogg was serious. He didn't want to stop until he reached Shanghai.

"To Shanghai we go then," said the captain, with a shrug of his shoulders.

The storm lasted all night, but the *Tankadere* survived it all. Next morning, Captain Bunsby proudly announced they were just one hundred miles from Shanghai.

A violent storm

It was going to be a close run thing. The steamer was due to leave Shanghai for Yokohama that evening.

And now the wind was dropping. By noon, the boat was forty miles from harbor and there was hardly a puff of wind in the air. Not long after, a thick fog descended. The *Tankadere* slowed to a snail's pace.

By 6:00 that evening they were still twenty miles from the harbor. There was no chance of catching the ship now.

Phileas Fogg was still perfectly calm, and yet at that moment, his twenty thousand pound wager seemed all but lost.

Just then, everyone on board heard the echoing hoot of an approaching ship. The next moment a tall funnel, billowing black smoke, came out of the fog about half a mile away.

"It's a steamer," shouted Captain Bunsby, swinging the ship's wheel around. The boats were on a collision course.

Phileas Fogg didn't hesitate. "Captain," he cried, "fire the alarm gun! Raise the distress flag."

The gun was fired and a crewman immediately raised the flag.

The ship, ghosting out of the fog, steamed on towards them . . .

Chapter 13
A Happy Reunion

It was lucky that the steamer had only just left port. It was still going at a slow pace. The distress flag was seen at the last minute and the steamer came to a halt, close to the *Tankadere*.

Almost everyone aboard the *Tankadere* cheered when they saw the name on the side of the steamer. Even Phileas Fogg allowed himself a brief smile.

It wasn't the steamer they had expected to see. It was the *Carnatic*! The very same ship that they had missed in Hong Kong! She had stopped at Shanghai to shelter during the storm. That was how the *Tankadere* had caught her up.

Phileas Fogg realized that there was no need to sail into Shanghai and catch the other steamer. The *Carnatic* would take them to Yokohama now. They were back on schedule.

Mr. Fogg gladly paid Captain Bunsby his bonus of two hundred pounds, and everyone went aboard the *Carnatic*. The only unhappy person was Detective Fix. He was the first to spot a very familiar face standing on deck. It was the missing traveler . . . Passepartout!

He had caught the *Carnatic* after all.

Fix went pale with worry, but he needn't have been concerned. Although, Passepartout glared icily at him, he wasn't ready to reveal to his master what the detective had told him.

Instead there was a joyous reunion between Passepartout, Phileas Fogg, and Aouda, who kissed the Frenchman on the cheek. Phileas Fogg warmly shook both his hands. He was happy to see his servant again.

"My dear man," said Mr. Fogg. "Where have you been? We looked everywhere before we left. We, of course, missed the *Carnatic* but we hoped that perhaps you had caught it."

"I didn't so much as catch it as stumble onto it," said Passepartout, looking straight at Fix.

Without mentioning Fix's name, Passepartout explained how he'd found out that the *Carnatic* was leaving earlier than expected; and how he was on his way to tell them the news when he was delayed by a stranger.

"He invited me for a drink," said Passepartout. "I've never drunk spirits in my life

A Happy Reunion

It was the Carnatic!

before, but he somehow managed to persuade me to have three whiskies."

Passepartout told how he eventually fell asleep. "When I awoke it was nearly time for the boat to leave. I just prayed you had found out that the ship was leaving early. So I dashed for the ship and made it just in time. Alas, you were not on board."

Phileas Fogg was the first to forgive his manservant. Both he and Aouda were just pleased to have their friend safely returned to them.

Passepartout caught up with Fix later that evening. He didn't waste a moment. "You got me drunk," he roared, "just to stop me warning my master that the ship was leaving early!"

With that, he charged straight at Fix, grabbed him by the collar and punched him hard, knocking him to the deck.

When Fix recovered, he stared coldly at Passepartout and said, "Have you finished?"

"For the time being," replied Passepartout. "Perhaps you will now believe that my master is an innocent traveler."

"Far from it," replied Fix. "I think he is a rascal and a robber. That's why I had to prevent you from telling him that the ship was leaving

"Where have you been?"

early. I had to keep him in Hong Kong until the warrant arrived."

Fix stared at Passepartout for a moment. "Will you tell Mr. Fogg what really happened now?"

"Why shouldn't I?" replied Passepartout.

"Because we have a common interest," said Fix. "Neither of us will know exactly what the truth is until we all get back to England, or Mr. Fogg makes a break for it either in Yokohama or America. So can we be friends until then without revealing anything to him?"

"We cannot be friends," said Passepartout, "but I will go along with your plan. Though if I see the first suggestion that you are trying to slow him down so he loses the bet, I will wring your neck like a chicken."

"Fair enough," said the detective. "I promise, but I will keep my eye on him in case he tries to do a vanishing trick."

The rest of the journey to Yokohama went without incident and they arrived on November 14. That same evening, the party, including Detective Fix, boarded the *General Grant* for the journey across the Pacific Ocean to San Francisco.

This steamship was by far the most powerful

He knocked Fix to the deck.

vessel on the Pacific run. Within a few days of leaving Yokohama, Phileas Fogg noted in his diary that, in distance, they had passed the halfway stage of the journey.

Mr. Fogg had taken more than fifty of the eighty days to do it, but that didn't worry him. The worst of the journey was over. The second half of the trip might be as long in miles, but it should be completed in a much faster time.

It was here, in the middle of the Pacific Ocean, that Phileas Fogg failed to notice something. He was always so precise and exact, but on this one occasion he had forgotten a vital rule of navigation.

Perhaps Mr. Fogg was paying too much attention to Aouda, and this is why he made the mistake. He was becoming quite enchanted with Aouda and spent as much time as possible with her.

Passepartout was certainly unaware what this momentous stage in their journey meant, so they all sailed blissfully on . . .

Eleven days later, on December 3, the *General Grant* entered the bay of the Golden Gate and reached San Francisco.

Give or take a few hours, Phileas Fogg was still on schedule.

Chapter 14
Danger at Medicine Bow

The next train from San Francisco to New York was due to leave at 6:00 that same evening.

The first thing that Phileas Fogg did on arriving in America was to change many of his English pound notes into dollars. Then, after having his passport stamped, he joined Passepartout and Aouda aboard a carriage for a tour of San Francisco.

Mr. Fogg still wasn't aware he was being followed by the familiar figure of Fix. The detective was determined not to lose sight of his man.

Late in the day, Passepartout spotted a gun shop. Its window was filled with the latest models of Colt pistols. He had heard about the Wild West, and troubles between settlers and native American Indian tribes.

"Perhaps we should buy some of those pistols," he suggested, "in case of trouble on our journey across America."

Phileas Fogg agreed and the Frenchman was allowed to take some money from the carpet-bag. He returned soon after with four pistols.

They arrived at the train station in good time. Fix, who had witnessed the purchase of the guns, was a little concerned. "What does Phileas Fogg want pistols for?" wondered the ever-suspicious detective.

The trans-continental railroad linking San Francisco and New York had only been completed two years earlier. It used to take at least

"Perhaps we should buy some pistols."

six months to cross America. Now the 3,786-mile railroad journey could be completed by train in seven days, if all went well.

Phileas Fogg thought he would be in New York by December 11, in good time to catch the Atlantic steamer for Liverpool, on England's west coast.

The train left San Francisco's Oakland Station promptly at 6:00 p.m. on December 3. It was already dark outside and starting to snow.

At 8:00 p.m. the lamps in the car were dimmed for the night. The swaying motion of the train, now speeding towards Sacramento, soon put everyone to sleep. The passengers snored their way through Sacramento at the midnight hour.

Beyond Sacramento, the train climbed into the Sierra Nevada. There was no sign of the sun the next morning. It was snowing heavily as the train wound its way through mountain passes, puffing smoke as it struggled upwards.

The train entered the State of Nevada by Carson Valley and pulled into Reno City at midday for a twenty minute stop, and lunch. Then it was off again for a hard afternoon's run.

All was going well until they came upon a herd of some twelve thousand bellowing buffalo crossing the railroad. The train was forced to stop.

Phileas Fogg wasn't very concerned, but Passepartout was anxious at the beasts delaying them. It was a huge herd and it took nearly four hours for them to cross the railroad.

The train traveled on. By 8:00 on the morning of December 5, they were in Utah, the land of the Great Salt Lake.

By December 6, the train was winding into the Rocky Mountains, past Fort Bridger, and into Wyoming territory.

The next day they were making good time when the locomotive suddenly came to a jarring halt, as it approached Medicine Bow.

Phileas Fogg looked out of the window. They had stopped on the approach to a huge old wooden bridge that crossed some rapids, hundreds of feet below.

He heard the conductor and locomotive engineer talking to another railroad man.

"No, you can't pass," the man was saying. "The bridge is very shaky. The last train only just made it. The bridge could collapse if another train went over."

By this time several of the passengers had got off the train, including Phileas Fogg. They

The train was forced to stop.

all gathered around the engineer, conductor, and the other man, who turned out to be the signalman at Medicine Bow.

"Isn't there any other alternative?" asked the conductor.

"No," said the signalman. "The only thing we can do is walk the passengers across and wait for another train to come in from the east."

The engineer spoke again. "Perhaps there is another way," he said. "I'm pretty sure that if all the passengers walked across and my load was lighter, I might just get the train across."

"But the bridge is very unsafe," urged the signalman.

"Maybe," said the engineer. "For sure, if the train crossed the bridge slowly, it might well bring it down. But going at speed is another matter."

The engineer reckoned that the bridge would undergo less stress if the train was going fast.

Phileas Fogg was doubtful about this bit of scientific argument, but he took the matter with his usual calm. So he and all the other passengers slowly walked across the bridge, to the other side.

Once across the bridge, Mr. Fogg sat down on a nearby rock and calmly looked at his

Danger at Medicine Bow

"The bridge is very shaky."

diary. Ignoring the train, he began to do some more calculations of how much time he had left, to finish his journey around the world.

Aouda and Passepartout anxiously watched the train, along with the other passengers.

The engineer got back into his cab and backed up the train for nearly a mile. Then he stopped to give the locomotive the chance to build up steam.

The locomotive hooted and the train jerked forward, slowly at first, then gathering speed. It belched black smoke, the wheels screaming for grip on the rails. The engineer saw the bridge ahead and put on the last bit of power he had . . .

Chapter 15
Ghost Town Gunfight

Everyone except Mr. Fogg watched, as the train approached the bridge at high speed. Passepartout crossed his fingers. Aouda hardly dared to look.

The train roared toward them at top speed. The bridge was just ahead. The passengers hid their eyes.

The train reached the bridge and raced onto it. The bridge creaked and shuddered dangerously. It was halfway across when suddenly, an ear-splitting crack was heard.

The passengers watched, as part of the bridge that the train had just crossed collapsed and fell into the rapids, far below.

To Passepartout, it seemed that the collapsing bridge was chasing the train. For every few yards the train traveled, a similar stretch of bridge collapsed behind it.

The bridge was starting to fall apart in concertina fashion, but the train thundered on.

At last the steaming locomotive was over! Then one by one, the cars behind it reached safety.

Just as the engineer slammed on his brakes, the rest of the bridge fell to pieces with a terrible crash.

The train came to a halt and the passengers cheered. Phileas Fogg looked up from his diary. "That was nothing to worry about, was it?" he said quietly.

Passepartout put a hand to his heart and shook his head.

"I don't know how you can be so calm, monsieur," he said.

The passengers rejoined the train and their journey continued on. That evening they passed Fort Saunders and Evans Pass, the highest point of the journey.

The next day before dawn, the train stopped at the old ghost town of Donald, to take on water. As the sun began to rise, Mr. Fogg decided to take a short walk. Snow had fallen, and everything looked crisp and white.

"You'd better be careful out there," warned the conductor. "Some of our passengers have been robbed in this old place."

Phileas Fogg wasn't concerned, but he did

The bridge was starting to fall apart.

take Passepartout, carrying the old green carpetbag. Fix joined them for company.

The town of Donald consisted of just a main street with some ramshackle old buildings on either side. The three men left the train and walked slowly down the street. They soon came to an old hotel. The doors at the front were swinging half off their hinges.

"Footprints!" cried Passepartout suddenly, pointing to the ground.

There were three sets of prints in the snow, all leading into the hotel.

"I think it's time we returned to the train," said Phileas Fogg matter-of-factly.

They had gone a few paces when a voice called after them, "Stop right there!"

Phileas Fogg, Passepartout, and Fix turned and saw that three men had appeared on the hotel steps. Each one had a pistol hanging in a holster at their hips.

"We don't want to stop your journey," said the first man, "but we'd be grateful if you would kindly leave that green carpetbag with us."

"There's nothing of any worth inside," said Passepartout.

"I'll decide that," said the man, stepping forward with his two companions. All three had

"You'd better be careful out there."

their hands on their guns, ready to draw and shoot.

Mr. Fogg quickly whispered to Passepartout and Fix. "Let them have the bag. I don't want anyone killed here. Our lives are more important."

The men moved closer. Suddenly Passepartout dropped the carpetbag and screamed out, "Draw!"

The three gunmen stopped in their tracks, each one pulling out their pistol as they did so.

Passepartout flicked back his jacket and surprised everyone by drawing his own gun with remarkable speed. Never was a gun drawn so quickly. And never were three shots fired so rapidly.

The first shot sent one gunman's hat flying. The next sent the second man's gun flying into the air. The last pierced the third man's shoulder. All three ran for their lives.

Phileas Fogg, for the first time in his life, was truly astounded. "When did you learn to shoot like that?" he asked.

"Remember my circus days, monsieur," Passepartout explained. "Yes, I rode elephants, but I was also a sharpshooter. I learned to shoot like that in the circus. I wasn't called

Never was a gun drawn so quickly.

Pistol Passepartout for nothing, monsieur."

"Well done, my man!" said Phileas Fogg.

"Wonderful!" said Fix, who was still shaking with fear. He had thought that his days as a London detective were about to end, in a backwater ghost town called Donald.

As it was, the danger wasn't over yet. Suddenly, they heard the voice of the conductor, shouting from the train.

"Everyone aboard!" he cried. "Quickly! We're being attacked by Indians!"

Phileas Fogg, Passepartout, and Fix raced for their lives.

Chapter 16
A Daring Attack

By the time Phileas Fogg, Passepartout, and Fix leapt aboard, the train was already moving away. The locomotive was belching black smoke as the engineer piled more fuel into the boiler, to gain speed.

A band of American Indian warriors on ponies were galloping alongside the train, as the locomotive struggled to get up speed. They were shooting wildly into the air with their guns.

Many of the passengers who had been carrying guns, were now firing out of the windows. Phileas Fogg, Passepartout, Fix, and even Aouda joined them. Phileas Fogg was glad that Passepartout had bought four guns in San Francisco.

The train consisted of the locomotive and fuel tender followed by the baggage car. Immediately behind the baggage car was the car carrying Phileas Fogg and his friends. The Indians' target was the baggage car.

Looking out of the window, Phileas Fogg saw four Indians leap off their ponies into the loco- motive's cab. He knew that there was a direct route from the baggage car, onto the fuel tender and locomotive. He decided to go to help the engineer and stoker.

"Come on!" he shouted, opening the door between his car and the baggage car. "Follow me!"

Passepartout and Fix followed him in. At exactly the same moment, three of the four Indians who had boarded the locomotive entered the baggage car at the other end.

The battle began. Phileas Fogg, Passepar- tout, and Fix advanced, dodging in and out of the crates and cases in the car, firing as they went. One Indian was wounded, and jumped from the train.

Suddenly, Fix was hit by a bullet and fell over. Passepartout fired again and hit another Indian.

Phileas Fogg realized it was too dangerous to remain in the baggage car. The Indians had the same idea. Both sides retreated, taking their wounded with them.

Safely back in their own car, Passepartout slammed the door shut and barricaded it with

A Daring Attack

They were galloping alongside the train.

some luggage. Luckily, Fix had only been grazed by the Indian's shot. Aouda attended to his wound.

By now the train was racing along at enormous speed, and many of the other attacking Indians were being left behind.

"Well, gentlemen," said Phileas Fogg. "The Indians have control of the locomotive. What are we going to do now?"

It was Passepartout who came up with the idea to unhook the locomotive and baggage car from the rest of the train.

The Indians have control.

"If we can do that," he said, "the Indians in the baggage car will be taken for a long ride, leaving us safely behind. There's no way they can stop the locomotive. They wouldn't know how to."

"Brilliant!" said Phileas Fogg. "But how do we uncouple the locomotive and baggage car?"

Passepartout came to the rescue again. "As well as an elephant rider and sharpshooter in the circus," he explained proudly, "I was also an acrobat!"

Passepartout thought that with a bit of luck he could get down between their car and the baggage car, and unhook them.

"It's too dangerous," said Mr. Fogg. "You'll kill yourself."

But Passepartout insisted. He opened the door that led to the baggage car and swiftly dropped down. He held on for grim life as the train raced on, swaying wildly from side to side.

They were still a few Indians riding alongside the train at top speed. They had all fired their guns, but now they were throwing spears and tomahawks at the train.

Soon Passepartout was under attack, as he hung upside down and struggled with the heavy irons linking the two cars. Mr. Fogg ordered him back, but he refused.

Passepartout had already undone all but one of the links. The last one was the main coupling arm. It was stuck fast and he couldn't move it, so he clambered across to the other side of the coupling. His feet were now on the baggage car side of the coupling.

The train went over a bend in the line and gave a huge jolt. All at once, the coupling jerked up and freed itself. The locomotive and baggage car, freed from the other cars, raced on alone.

Phileas Fogg was about to let out a cheer, when he realized the terrible situation Passepartout had left himself in. He was still clinging onto the baggage car, moving farther and farther away from his friends.

Passepartout had no chance. He disappeared into the distance with the runaway locomotive and baggage car.

The others cars did exactly as Passepartout had planned. They slowly came to a halt. The passengers found themselves just a few yards from a station called Fort Kearney. Several had been wounded in the attack, but none fatally.

Aouda was safe and Phileas Fogg, despite being in the thick of it, had not received a scratch. He got out of the train and looked

A Daring Attack

He disappeared into the distance.

down the track to see the last of the Indians still chasing the locomotive and baggage car.

"I will not leave here," cried Phileas Fogg, "until I have found Passepartout, alive or dead!"

"You are a good man," answered Aouda, with tears in her eyes.

She knew that it would mean the end to his challenge. If he stayed behind to search for Passepartout, he would never reach New York in time to catch the steamer.

Fort Kearney was home to a small U.S. cavalry unit. It stood on high ground, nearly a mile away. The lookout must have seen the Indians and the runaway train, because a party of thirty cavalry riders arrived soon after.

The commanding officer introduced himself as Captain Rogers.

"Good to see you, captain," said Mr. Fogg. "We've lost a man; he's probably a prisoner of the Indians now. His life is at risk and we must pursue them!"

Captain Rogers quickly agreed to give chase and asked Phileas Fogg to come with them. They had a spare horse for him. Fix, injured as he was, stepped forward and volunteered to go too.

"I'd rather you stay with Aouda and keep her safe," said Phileas Fogg.

The detective was very uneasy, as the last thing he wanted was to see his man ride into the snow and vanish forever. But he could not argue with Mr. Fogg's request.

So Fix and Aouda anxiously watched them go.

Chapter 17
Train Whistles and Cavalry Bugles

Phileas Fogg and the cavalry disappeared into the snowy white distance. Silence fell on Fort Kearney train station. No one said a word. Some of the passengers were terrified that the Indians would return.

After about an hour, they heard the faint sound of a locomotive whistle coming from the east. Everyone looked down the track. The whistle grew louder. At last, a black shadow emerged from the snowstorm.

It was the missing locomotive with the baggage car still attached to it. It slowed, and was linked once more to the other passenger cars.

The passengers cheered as the engineer and his stoker appeared. They explained what had happened. The Indians had knocked them unconscious and when they awoke, all their

Phileas Fogg and the cavalry disappeared.

attackers had gone. The train had stopped because the boiler fire had gone out.

"The Indians must have left us for dead after robbing the baggage car," said the engineer. "So we decided we had better light another fire and get back to you."

Aouda was desperate for any news of Passepartout. Neither man had seen him. "He must have been taken by the Indians," said the engineer.

Aouda then begged them to hold the train until Phileas Fogg returned.

"It's impossible," said the engineer, sternly. "We cannot risk the passengers being attacked again. We have to go."

"When is the next train to New York?" asked Aouda.

"Tomorrow evening," replied the engineer.

"That will be too late!" she cried. "You must wait!"

"Madam," said the engineer. "If you wish to travel with us, you must get aboard now."

"I cannot," said the brave Aouda.

Fix agreed with her, of course. He wasn't going to leave his man behind.

All the other passengers had boarded the train and the engineer sounded his whistle.

The train slowly began to leave the station. Just as it did, the conductor appeared at an open door and dropped down the few possessions that belonged to Phileas Fogg's party.

The old green carpetbag, and its valuable hoard of dollars and pound notes, was among them. At least the Indians hadn't taken that!

Fix and Aouda shivered in the station office, and watched the train slowly disappear. At midday the snow stopped falling and a faint sun appeared high in the sky. Now the wind began to rise, and with it came the sound of distant bugles.

Aouda and Fix leapt to their feet and saw an amazing sight. A lone bareback rider on an Indian pony was racing down the hill toward the station. And behind that rider came a single column of cavalry.

Aouda and Fix recognized Phileas Fogg at the head of the column, alongside Captain Rogers. At first, Aouda thought that the cavalry must be chasing the Indian rider. But as the figure came closer, it gradually dawned on her who it was.

The rider pulled up right in front of her in a cloud of dust. It was dear Passepartout!

Aouda threw herself into Passepartout's arms

and kissed him on the cheek. There was a kiss for Mr. Fogg too. They were the two bravest men she had ever met! Phileas Fogg was definitely the shyest too. He couldn't stop blushing at such an outburst of affection from Aouda.

Fix stood and stared at Phileas Fogg. He never thought he would see him again.

"We had just reached the Indian camp, when we saw Passepartout escaping on the horse," explained Mr. Fogg. "And as soon as the Indians saw the cavalry, they vanished."

"But riding bareback like an Indian, Passepartout!" cried Aouda. "How on earth did you manage that?"

"It was nothing," said Passeportout. "When I was in the circus I was also taught to be a bareback rider."

"Is there anything you can't do?" laughed Phileas Fogg.

Passepartout was actually the only person who wished that Mr. Fogg hadn't come looking for him.

"It's cost you dearly, monsieur," he said quietly. "You stayed behind to save me, and it means the bet is lost. We can never get to New York in time now."

Passepartout desperately tried to think of

a way out of the problem. He started looking around the station and returned a few minutes later.

"Our train only left here about an hour ago, didn't it?" he asked.

"True," answered Phileas Fogg. "But we are unlikely to catch it on foot."

"We might catch our train by sled though," replied Passepartout. "Especially a sled with sails."

"A sled!" laughed Mr. Fogg. "Where would we find one of those out here in the wilderness?"

"Just follow me," replied Passepartout.

A puzzled Phileas Fogg followed his manservant to the back of the platform office. There stood a large wooden sled with enough room for at least four people. It had a tall mast and a sail flapping from it. At the back was a rudder to steer with.

The sled had been kept at the station to help passengers get to the fort when the snow was too deep to use horses.

"Don't tell me you were a sled driver during your time with the circus," smiled Mr. Fogg affectionately.

"No," said Passepartout, "but it shouldn't be

impossible for us to teach ourselves how to sail it."

Phileas Fogg agreed. He asked some of the cavalrymen to tow the sled to the top of a nearby hill. Then they all got aboard.

Mr. Fogg took up his position beside the steering rudder. Aouda sat beside him. Passepartout and Fix sat in the middle and unfurled the huge sail.

The cavalrymen gave a push and the sled began to slide down the hill. The wind filled the sails and the sled raced away.

What a machine! The wind pushed it along with such power that Passepartout had difficulty hanging onto the ropes that guided the sail. Phileas Fogg hung onto the rudder for his life. They sped across the fresh snow at great speed.

The distance between Fort Kearney and Omaha, the next big city on the train's route, was around two hundred miles.

Phileas Fogg judged that if the wind held up, the sled could keep going at around forty miles an hour. They could make Omaha in five hours.

The train had several stops to make on the way. The sled could keep going. The train also had to follow the winding track. The sled could take a more direct route.

"If nothing breaks," shouted Phileas Fogg

What a machine!

from the rudder, "we might just beat the train to Omaha."

They crossed the frozen River Platte and left the railroad and its twisting track alongside the river. Phileas Fogg's route was to be a straight line to Omaha.

Night fell as the sled and its human cargo sped across the carpet of snow. Phileas Fogg steered by the gleam of the moonlight, while Passepartout and Fix took turns holding the ropes that guided the sail.

The journey went like magic and the sled slithered to a halt outside Omaha train station just as their train pulled in.

Phileas Fogg and his party joined the other passengers. Passepartout was given a hero's welcome. After all, he was the man who had saved all their lives by freeing the locomotive during the attack.

Without further disasters or adventures, the train set off for Chicago, arriving there the next day.

It was another nine hundred miles from Chicago to New York and Phileas Fogg was still a little behind time.

Luckily, the train engineer knew all about Mr. Fogg and his wager. He piled on the coal

Slithering to a halt outside the station

as never before and the train roared across Indiana, Ohio, and Pennsylvania. At last it crossed the New Jersey state line.

At 11:15 p.m. on December 11, the train finally pulled into New York harbor, right beside the Cunard Line pier.

The *China*, the steamer due to take Phileas Fogg and his companions to Liverpool in England, had steamed out of New York just forty-five minutes earlier.

Chapter 18
Phileas Fogg the Pirate

Forty-five minutes late! Passepartout was almost in tears. He thought of all the incidents during the journey where they might have saved that small amount of time.

Phileas Fogg, as usual, blamed no one for the situation. He seemed almost relaxed about it all. "There has to be another boat leaving New York," he said, looking around the harbor.

Mr. Fogg spotted a small trading vessel with smoke billowing from the funnel; a sure sign it was about to leave. He hurried across and found himself beside the *Henrietta*, an iron-hulled boat with a wooden upper structure. He jumped aboard and asked to see the captain.

A big man of about fifty years with a weather-beaten face appeared. "I am Andrew Speedy, captain of this vessel," he announced.

Phileas Fogg introduced himself and asked when the *Henrietta* was going to sea.

"In an hour," said the old sea salt.

"Where are you bound for?"

"For Bordeaux, in France," was the reply.

"Would you change course for Liverpool, for a price?" asked Mr. Fogg.

"For Liverpool!" gasped the skipper in astonishment. "I might as well go to China."

Phileas Fogg ignored the remark. "Money is no object," he said. "I will pay the owner whatever he wants."

"I am the owner," said Captain Speedy.

"Then I will buy the boat from you," said Mr. Fogg.

"No, you won't!" cried Captain Speedy. "I love this boat too much to part with her."

Phileas Fogg changed his approach. "Will you carry me and my three friends to Bordeaux for two hundred dollars each?"

"Not for two thousand dollars each," said the man.

"Then four thousand dollars each," appealed Mr. Fogg.

Captain Speedy scratched his head and then smiled. "I'm leaving right now. I'll take you!"

Now it was Phileas Fogg's turn to smile. It wasn't just that he was happy to have found a boat. He seemed to be plotting something as well.

"I am Andrew Speedy, captain of this vessel."

Phileas Fogg and his companions went aboard and almost immediately, the *Henrietta* raised anchor and steamed out toward the Atlantic.

Passepartout almost fainted when he heard how much Phileas Fogg had paid for the voyage. Mr. Fix just hung his head. His share of the reward for recovering the money was getting smaller by the day.

***

The next morning the *Henrietta* was heading out into the Atlantic. At the ship's wheel was a man looking remarkably like Phileas Fogg. And indeed, it was him.

Captain Speedy's voice could now be heard shouting and screaming from a cabin below decks. That is where Mr. Fogg had locked him up.

Phileas Fogg had asked to be taken to Bordeaux, but that was just his excuse. In the first few hours of the voyage he had bribed every member of the crew with his dollars and pound notes to mutiny and take the ship to Liverpool instead of Bordeaux!

This was piracy on the high seas, but Phileas Fogg wasn't worried a jot.

He estimated that the *Henrietta* could cross the Atlantic in about nine days. They might just be in Liverpool by the morning of December 21, the day the wager was due.

The first few days went well. The wind was from the northeast and the sails were put up to increase the engine speed. The *Henrietta* was ploughing across the Atlantic at the speed of a genuine transatlantic steamer.

Fix knew nothing about the bribing of the crew. He was told that the captain was very ill and that Phileas Fogg was doing his job.

Fix's suspicious mind was now thinking that Mr. Fogg was not going to Liverpool at all. Perhaps he was taking the ship to some pirate island, where he could live happily for the rest of his life.

On December 13, a storm set in. It blew for three days. The *Henrietta* made slow progress in the gigantic seas.

By December 16, the weather was better. The worst had passed—or so the travelers thought.

The next morning, the chief engineer approached Mr. Fogg. "I'm sorry sir," he said, "it looks as though we'll not have enough coal to reach England. We have been pushing the boat too hard."

Phileas Fogg thought for a moment and then ordered the engineer to keep burning the coal until the supply was exhausted. The *Henrietta* continued to race toward England. But that afternoon the engineer prepared to put on his very last bit of fuel.

"Don't let the fires go out!" ordered Mr. Fogg. "Let them burn to the last cinder."

As the ship finally started to slow, Mr. Fogg told Passepartout to free Captain Speedy.

"It'll be like freeing a madman for sure," said Passepartout, nervously.

Phileas Fogg was at the ship's wheel.

The job was done and Captain Speedy appeared on deck.

"Where are we?" he shouted, his face purple with anger.

Phileas Fogg was calm as always. "Captain Speedy, we are now some seven hundred miles from Liverpool."

"You pirate!" shouted Speedy.

"Pirate or not," said Phileas Fogg, "I would now like to buy this boat from you."

"No!" screamed Speedy. "By all the devils, no!"

"Then I shall have to burn her!"

"Burn the *Henrietta*!" exploded Speedy.

"Yes," said Mr. Fogg, "well, at least the upper half. We have run out of coal and need wood to burn."

"Burn my ship!" cried Speedy. "A vessel worth fifty thousand dollars!"

"I have sixty thousand dollars right here," said Phileas Fogg, reaching into his bag and producing a huge wad of notes.

The size of the bounty in Mr. Fogg's hand very quickly changed Captain Speedy's mind. He knew his boat was only worth one third of that amount. Sixty thousand dollars was a great bargain.

Burning the boat

So the deal was agreed.

When Captain Speedy had pocketed the money, Phileas Fogg revealed to him the story of the wager.

Speedy began to laugh. "Sir," he said, "I have gained some forty thousand dollars in profit for this old boat, so I am very happy. But I have also decided that I like you, Mr. Fogg. You have something of the American in you! I'd like to see you win your wager."

"I thank you, sir," replied Phileas Fogg. "So shall we start by removing all the interior seats, bunks, and frames to burn? That will keep us going a mile or two!"

That evening they burned them all. The next day, December 19, the masts, rafts, and spars were all fed into the boiler fires.

The wooden railings, the fittings, and the greater part of the deck disappeared the next day, December 20.

And on that day, they sighted Ireland.

Chapter 19
England!

That evening the *Henrietta*, desperately short of fuel, was just off Queenstown, a small harbor on the south coast of Ireland.

Phileas Fogg had just twenty-two hours and forty-five minutes left to finish his journey. And he knew that he was running out of time.

Mr. Fogg, however, had an idea. He knew that Queenstown was the Irish port where the transatlantic steamers often dropped off mail for quick delivery to England.

This mail was carried by express trains from Queenstown to Dublin, and on from there by the fastest boats to Liverpool. It was said that the mail usually reached England twelve hours ahead of the Atlantic steamers.

Phileas Fogg asked Captain Speedy to change course and head for Queenstown. It was a desperate last gamble, and it only just worked. The boat, burning the very last piece of wood, entered the harbor at 1:00 a.m.

"Goodbye and good luck!"

Mr. Fogg, Passepartout, Detective Fix, and Aouda leapt off the ship and raced for the Dublin train.

"Goodbye and good luck!" shouted Captain Speedy, who was standing on the skeleton remains of the iron hull of his ship. There was very little else left of it. The boiler had consumed every piece of wood.

Phileas Fogg and his friends boarded the train just as it was leaving the station.

By dawn they were in Dublin. Within the hour they were on the fast steamer for Liverpool, where they got ashore at 11:40 a.m.

Phileas Fogg was now only six hours distant by rail from London, with just under nine hours to spare. He was now sure he could win his bet.

Fix was also sure of something. On arriving at Liverpool, he had dashed off to the nearest police station and finally got the arrest warrant he had been after, ever since the beginning of the journey.

Fix returned and put his hand on Mr. Fogg's shoulder, and said the fatal words, "Mr. Phileas Fogg I have a warrant for your arrest for the robbery of fifty-five thousand pounds from the Bank of England."

England!

When Passepartout saw his master arrested, he could have killed Fix on the spot. Thankfully, Aouda held him back.

Passepartout was heartbroken. If his master was an honest man, he would be ruined by losing the bet. If he truly was the bank robber —and Passepartout couldn't bear to think that —then he would spend many years in prison.

Phileas Fogg was taken to a local prison cell, where he sat on a bench calmly contemplating

Sitting in a prison cell

his situation. He had been utterly surprised at his arrest. Yet, strangely, he had not given up. To Mr. Fogg, hope never died.

Later that morning he took out his diary and wrote: *Saturday, December 21, Liverpool, eightieth day, 1:45 p.m. Seven hours left.*

An hour later he wrote down: *2:45 p.m. Six hours left.*

At 2:47 p.m. he heard the sound of running feet. Suddenly, the cell door clanged open. It was Fix, followed by Passepartout and Aouda.

Fix was almost out of breath. "Sir, forgive me," he gasped. "A most unfortunate mistake . . . most unfortunate likeness . . . the real robber was arrested three days ago . . . you are free to go!"

Phileas Fogg walked up to Fix and proceeded to knock him to the floor with a single blow to the chin.

"Well hit, monsieur!" cried an absolutely delighted Passepartout, as Phileas Fogg left the prison cell, proudly holding his head high in the air.

The party rushed to Liverpool station and boarded a fast train for London. The train was due in London at 8:35 p.m. The wager was still on!

Excitement mounted as the train raced south. The counties of Cheshire, Warwickshire, and Buckinghamshire flashed past outside, as Passepartout held his breath with excitement.

The train steamed into the outskirts of London and began to slow as it approached the end of its journey.

Now the station was just half a mile away. Phileas Fogg remained sitting quietly by himself. Passepartout and Aouda, unable to contain their excitement, leaned out of the window.

The station was just in sight, and Passe-par-tout whooped with excitement. "We're almost there!" he shouted.

Just then a green signal turned to red. The train suddenly jammed on its brakes and came to an abrupt halt!

Passepartout saw a railroad guard standing beside the red signal that had stopped the train. "Why have we stopped?" he asked, leaning out of the window.

"You'll have to wait for the Glasgow train," he replied. "It's late leaving the station. Your train can't go into the station until the Glasgow one is on its way."

Phileas Fogg thought about getting out of

"Why have we stopped?"

the train and running to the station. But it was still too far away to make it in time.

They just sat there as the minutes ticked away. Passepartout's and Aouda's expressions became more desperate as each moment passed.

At last the train began moving again and, a few moments later, pulled into the station.

As Mr. Fogg stepped off the train, the large hand of the station clock moved. The time was now 8:50 p.m. He was already five minutes late.

Aouda burst into tears. Passepartout was heartbroken.

Yet even at that most terrible of moments, Phileas Fogg managed to smile at his bad luck. "All the way around the world," he said, "and now I'm just five minutes late."

Phileas Fogg had lost his wager!

Chapter 20
The Final Race

That evening, an air of sadness hung over Mr. Fogg's London home. Phileas Fogg knew he was financially ruined—ruined by a glory-seeking, bumbling detective. Fix had robbed him of the vital hours he spent in prison.

The first thing Passepartout had done on arriving home was to rush upstairs and turn off his gaslight, which had been burning the whole time he was away.

He had already found a gas account in the mailbox. He wasn't brave enough to open it. The account would be for far more than he could pay.

Aouda sat looking at Phileas Fogg, wondering where her future lay now. She felt very sorry indeed for her friend and protector.

Nobody spoke much the next morning. The only conversation was between Phileas Fogg and Passepartout. The loyal servant wanted to take the blame for allowing Fix's identity to stay secret for so long.

Turning off his gaslight

Phileas Fogg did not blame Passepartout. He said he would have probably done the same in Passepartout's position.

"For all you knew," laughed Phileas Fogg, "I could have been the bank robber!"

The hours passed slowly. Mr. Fogg had decided to go the Reform Club later that night, to hand over the twenty thousand pounds to his companions.

At 7:30 p.m. he went to speak with Aouda in her room.

"I was counting on giving you part of my fortune to help you settle in London," he said, "but now I am ruined."

"I know," said Aouda, calmly. "But you've been kind enough to me already. I have you to thank for my life. I am more worried about what will become of you, Mr. Fogg."

"I'll be all right," said Phileas Fogg. "I am in need of nothing. I have nothing."

"What!" exclaimed Aouda, "No family, nor friends?"

"No," replied Phileas Fogg, matter-of-factly.

Aouda looked affectionately at Mr. Fogg. "They do say, sir, that loneliness is best shared by two people."

Phileas Fogg thought that was a wonderful

way of saying something special. But he wasn't ready for what came next.

"I wonder, Mr. Fogg," said Aouda, taking his hand. "I wonder if I might suggest an alternative to loneliness."

"An alternative?" Phileas Fogg was puzzled.

Aouda said it without hesitation. "Will you marry me?"

For once in his life, Phileas Fogg lost his calm. But despite the shock, he knew his answer.

"Dear Aouda, perhaps you knew it all along," he said, trembling. "Perhaps you didn't. But, yes, I do love you. I loved you from the moment I saw you."

"Then what's your answer to my proposal of marriage?" she asked.

Phileas Fogg blushed and then smiled. "The answer, of course, is 'Yes'."

Passepartout was summoned and told the good news. He was absolutely delighted.

"Who needs money, monsieur," he cried, "when you have love!"

He was immediately sent off to see the minister at the nearest church. Phileas Fogg wanted to get married the very next day.

***

"Will you marry me?"

It was 8:15 p.m. when Passepartout left the house to find the minister. He knew the time because he had just looked at his pocket watch. It was 8:20 p.m. by the time he knocked on the minister's door.

He explained his mission to the minister. "My master wants to marry tomorrow," he said.

"Tomorrow!" exclaimed the minister. "That would be impossible. I'm far too busy. It is a Sunday after all!"

"Sunday!" cried Passepartout. "It can't be. It's Monday tomorrow."

"You seem to be confused, sir," replied the minister. "I promise you that tomorrow is Sunday. Today is Saturday."

Passepartout was utterly puzzled. "Are you absolutely sure it's Saturday?" he asked.

"Of course I am!" answered the minister.

Passepartout stood frozen to the spot for a moment, wondering what to do. It was as if he had been hit by a thunderbolt.

The next moment Passepartout looked at his watch, spun around, and hurtled off down the street. He sprinted home to Phileas Fogg's house like a man possessed.

Passepartout, his hair flying in every direction and his hat missing, flew through his master's door at 8:32 p.m. Seizing his master by the collar, he dragged him out into the street, calling on Aouda to follow.

"No time to explain!" he cried breathlessly. "We must get to the Reform Club this instant! Cab!"

A horse-drawn cab pulled up beside them. Passepartout hauled his master and Aouda inside and slammed the door. "To the Reform Club!" cried the Frenchman. "Quickly. Our lives depend on it!"

The horse and cab raced away.

Passepartout now had a few moments to explain what had happened.

"It's a complete mystery to me, Mr. Fogg," he gasped, "the minister says it's still Saturday . . . Saturday, December 21, not Sunday, December 22! I don't understand, but the minister can't be wrong. We can still get to the club in time if we are lucky."

"It can't be Saturday," gasped Phileas Fogg.

"The minister wouldn't lie," said Passepartout.

Then Phileas Fogg began to smile. Stunned as he was after being kidnapped from his own house, the answer to the puzzle hit him. It was a puzzle which had an answer in the middle of the mighty Pacific Ocean.

Phileas Fogg looked at his watch. It was now 8:36 p.m. He shouted at the driver. "Cabbie! Five hundred pounds if you can get me to the Reform Club in nine minutes. Any later than 8:45 p.m. and I won't be able to pay you a penny. I shall be bankrupt!"

The final race was on! The cabbie cracked the whip above his horse's head as if he was competing in the Kentucky Derby. The cab horse galloped off at a frightening speed. It raced around bends, leaving the cab balancing on one wheel.

"No time to explain!"

Passepartout rather wished he'd stayed behind. The journey seemed more dangerous than the worst storms in the South China Sea; and more terrifying than the Indian attack.

Having overturned two coal carts and a baker's van, the cab finally lost a wheel and jolted to a violent stop. The Reform Club was still two streets away.

"Run for it, monsieur!" shouted Passepartout.

Poor Passepartout was out of breath. He and Aouda watched as Phileas Fogg leapt out of the cab and sprinted down the road towards the club.

There was no doubting it. Mr. Fogg was running faster than he had ever run in his life.

Chapter 21
At the Reform Club

The Reform Club had heard little news of Phileas Fogg since he'd departed on his voyage around the world and then sent them a telegraph message from Italy, saying he was on his way to Suez.

There had been lots of talk about him, and telegraph messages had been dispatched around the world to try and find further news of him. Was he dead? Had he abandoned his journey? Would he appear before 8:45 p.m. on Saturday, December 21?

There had also been rumors that he was wanted for robbing the Bank of England of fifty-five thousand pounds. But Scotland Yard was not prepared to confirm that story because their man Fix had seemed to have disappeared too.

On the evening of Saturday, December 21, the men who had taken the bet with Mr. Fogg — Jeremy Ralph, John Sullivan, and Tom Flanagan —were waiting at the Reform Club.

"The fact is," said Flanagan, "Mr. Fogg's wager was utterly foolish. He could never have got round the world in eighty days."

"He won't turn up now," said Ralph.

"It's 8:41 p.m.," said Sullivan.

"Just four minutes more," said Ralph, excitedly.

No one could keep their eyes off the clock. The big hand of the club's ancient clock moved again. It was now 8:42 p.m.

"Mind you," said Sullivan. "Mr. Fogg is always very punctual. You can tell the time of day by his comings and goings. He never likes to arrive either early or late."

The big arm clicked again . . . 8:43 p.m.

The mood was tense. There was complete silence in the club, except for the ticking of the clock.

Sullivan jumped nervously as one of the more ancient of club members suddenly started snoring. It was 8:44 p.m.

"Just sixty seconds to go," squeaked Flanagan.

Now they all watched the smallest dial on the clock where a tiny hand counted off the seconds.

Sullivan breathed out a huge sigh. The seconds ticked away. No one dared say a word.

Waiting at the Reform Club

Thirty seconds . . . forty seconds . . . fifty seconds . . .

At 8:44 p.m. and fifty seconds, there was the sound of voices outside as someone ran up the steps toward the club's front door.

At fifty-five seconds, the front door was heard to open.

At fifty-eight seconds the door to the main club room swung open with a crash. An exhausted and gasping man appeared from behind it.

"Good evening, gentlemen," puffed Mr. Fogg, out of breath after his desperate run from the cab. "Two seconds early by my watch, I think!"

There was a stunned silence in the Reform Club for almost a minute.

Sullivan spoke first. "Phileas Fogg, I knew you were a punctual man, but isn't this cutting it a bit fine?"

Laughter broke out around the room.

"I was not punctual at all," admitted Phileas Fogg, catching his breath at last. "In fact, I only have Passepartout my servant and Aouda my friend, to thank for my being here on time."

At that moment Passepartout's head peered around the door. He too was still out of breath.

"Come in, dear Passepartout," said Mr. Fogg.

"Good evening, gentlemen."

Passepartout came in, followed by Aouda. Only then did Phileas Fogg reveal the mystery of the different dates.

"What a fool I was," he began. "I should have known all along that we arrived back a day earlier than we thought. If Aouda and I hadn't decided to marry . . ."

Phileas Fogg had to stop speaking as a great round of applause from the other members exploded around the room. He was very moved.

"Yes, we are to marry," he continued, raising his hand for silence. "You are very kind, but let me continue with my story. If Aouda and I hadn't decided to marry and Passepartout hadn't gone to see the minister I would never have realized my mistake."

Mr. Fogg wiped a bead of sweat from his brow and continued. "When Passepartout came rushing home like a madman, my mistake slowly dawned on me."

"Mistake, monsieur?" asked Passepartout, still completely puzzled.

Phileas Fogg went on. "The sun rises in the east. So, as we were traveling around the world in an easterly direction, we were chasing the sun all the time, gaining a little time every day."

Passepartout interrupted for a moment. "But,

monsieur, we couldn't have gained a whole day, could we?"

"We certainly did," said Mr. Fogg. "By the time we reached the middle of the Pacific Ocean, we had gained a whole twenty-four hours."

"The dateline!" interrupted John Sullivan excitedly. "The international dateline in the middle of the Pacific Ocean. That's where travelers going around the world in an easterly direction finally gain a complete day!"

"Exactly!" said Phileas Fogg. "We reached that line on a Saturday. And, of course, once you cross the line, the twenty-four hours of that day start all over again. In other words, we had two Saturdays."

"Bravo!" cried several of the club members, some pretending that they understood it all, even if they didn't.

Flanagan did understand it. "So instead of arriving in Liverpool on Saturday, December 21," he said, "it was really Friday, December 20, a whole day earlier than you thought!"

"Precisely!" said Phileas Fogg.

"Well," said Flanagan, "three cheers for Passepartout!"

The Reform Club had never heard such loud cheers.

That evening in the club, there were great celebrations to mark both the winning of the wager and Mr. Fogg's coming marriage.

Ralph, Sullivan, and Flanagan were not upset at losing their bet. They were wealthy men and would have no problem paying the twenty thousand pounds. They were just happy to see Phileas Fogg safely returned.

***

So, Phileas Fogg had won his twenty thousand pound wager, and forty-eight hours later he and Aouda were married. Mr. Fogg was pleased to have won his bet, but he was a great deal happier to have won his bride.

Money had never been the object of Phileas Fogg taking the wager. He only wanted to prove that the journey was possible in eighty days. The achievement was more important to him than the money.

In any case, he had already spent nineteen thousand pounds in costs during the journey. He had also promised Passepartout one thousand pounds as a present for his help during the journey.

So Phileas Fogg had won twenty thousand

"Three cheers for Passepartout!"

pounds and paid out twenty thousand pounds. Yet, he was far richer in many other ways than when he left England.

Phileas Fogg, with Aouda beside him, had become the happiest of men. As Passepartout had once told him, "Who needs money, monsieur, when you can have love."

Passepartout had become a very cheerful Frenchman too. And it wasn't just because his master was getting married.

No. With Mr. Fogg's present of one thousand pounds, Passepartout now had enough money to pay his gas account!

The End